GLOSSARY

D0980245

Here are some *Clone Wars* terms that might help you along the way.

Blaster: The main weapon used in the galaxy.

Clone troopers: Physically identical soldiers bred and trained to serve in the Galactic Republic's army.

Crab droid: A six-legged droid that moves from side to side like a crab.

Destroyer droid: A droid that can transform into a wheel and roll about.

Droid: A robot or android.

Galactic Republic: The government that rules the galaxy.

Hologram: A projected image of a person.

Jedi: Masters of the Force. They use their power to protect the Republic.

Senator: A representative of the Galactic Republic.

Separatist Alliance: The group trying to take over the Galactic Republic.

STAR WARS®

THE CLONE WARS™

BOMBAD JEDI

Adapted by Rob Valois

Based on the TV series *STAR WARS: THE CLONE WARS*

Grosset & Dunlap • LucasBooks

GROSSET & DUNLAP
Published by the Penguin Group
Penguin Group (USA) Inc., 375 Hudson Street, New York, New York 10014, USA
Penguin Group (Canada), 90 Eglinton Avenue East, Suite 700,
Toronto, Ontario M4P 2Y3, Canada
(a division of Pearson Penguin Canada Inc.)
Penguin Books Ltd., 80 Strand, London WC2R 0RL, England
Penguin Group Ireland, 25 St. Stephen's Green, Dublin 2, Ireland
(a division of Penguin Books Ltd.)
Penguin Group (Australia), 250 Camberwell Road,
Camberwell, Victoria 3124, Australia
(a division of Pearson Australia Group Pty. Ltd.)
Penguin Books India Pvt. Ltd., 11 Community Centre,
Panchsheel Park, New Delhi—110 017, India
Penguin Group (NZ), 67 Apollo Drive, Rosedale, North Shore 0632, New Zealand
(a division of Pearson New Zealand Ltd.)
Penguin Books (South Africa) (Pty.) Ltd., 24 Sturdee Avenue,
Rosebank, Johannesburg 2196, South Africa

Penguin Books Ltd., Registered Offices:
80 Strand, London WC2R 0RL, England

This book is published in partnership with LucasBooks, a division of Lucasfilm Ltd.

Library of Congress Control Number: 2008024121

ISBN: 978-0-448-45038-4   10 9 8 7 6 5 4 3 2

CHAPTER 1

Jar Jar Binks jumped up and down. Everyone was looking at a very important holographic message and he couldn't see anything. C-3PO's big, shiny head always seemed to be in his way. No matter how hard Jar Jar tried, he just couldn't see anything but golden metal. It wasn't fair.

Jar Jar, C-3PO, and Senator Padmé Amidala were on an important diplomatic mission. The Senator from the planet of Rodia in the Outer

Rim of the galaxy had asked to meet with Padmé. He was an old family friend, so Padmé felt comfortable meeting with him without an escort of clone troopers.

The holographic message was from Chancellor Palpatine, the head of the Galactic Republic. He was concerned that Padmé hadn't brought any clone troopers along. The galaxy was at war and it was unsafe for a Senator to travel without guards.

Hearing this, Jar Jar pushed his way past C-3PO. "Yousa no needin' to worry, Chancellor. As representative of Naboo, I . . ." Jar Jar was going to say that he would protect Padmé, but just then he tripped over C-3PO's chair and fell headfirst right through the hologram. As he tried to catch himself, he reached out and slammed several of the buttons on the control panel of Padmé's starship.

"Jar Jar, look out!" Padmé yelled, but it was too late.

The ship rocked back and forth, knocking C-3PO out of his chair. "What is happening?!" he called out as his metal body smashed against the floor. A moment later, Jar Jar came crashing down on top of him.

Padmé quickly grabbed the controls and stopped the ship from rocking. She looked over at the hologram. The Chancellor appeared concerned. "May I recommend that only those who are *qualified* for these delicate peace talks participate in them," he said.

The Chancellor meant that he didn't think that Jar Jar was qualified to help with the peace talks. Jar Jar knew that he was smart enough to help. It wasn't his fault that he was sometimes a little clumsy. Jar Jar, who was still sitting on C-3PO, looked up at Padmé. He could tell that she agreed with the Chancellor.

CHAPTER 2

The ship landed in a hangar in the tropical rain forest of Rodia. The area was one big swamp, just like where Jar Jar was born. His people were called Gungans and they were from a planet named Naboo. Naboo had many large oceans and swamps, and that was where Jar Jar had lived until he met Padmé Amidala and became a representative of Naboo in the Galactic Senate.

Jar Jar wanted to help with the negotiations,

but Padmé said that he should stay behind and keep an eye on C-3PO because he was always getting into trouble.

"Trouble? Me? Really?" C-3PO said, not knowing what Padmé was talking about. It wasn't C-3PO who was always getting into trouble! It was Jar Jar!

"Meesa understand, my lady," Jar Jar replied in a sad voice. He felt bad that he wasn't going along with her.

He said good-bye to Padmé and then he and

C-3PO went down to the hangar to look at the swamp. From deep within the strange-looking plants and trees they could hear a lot of weird animal noises. Jar Jar couldn't recognize any of them.

"How rude!" C-3PO suddenly said. He could understand what the animals were saying. As a protocol droid, it was his job to translate different languages. C-3PO could speak over six million different ones.

"Whaten dey speakin'?" Jar Jar asked, wanting to know what they were saying.

"I couldn't possibly repeat it," C-3PO
replied. His cheeks would have been red with
embarrassment if they had been able to change
color.

Jar Jar looked out into the muddy water and
said, "Ah, theesa swamp dwellers just lika meesa.
I will convince them of our good fellowship."

He wanted to make friends with the swamp
creatures.

C-3PO moved nervously. "Do be careful, Jar
Jar. I don't think they are quite like your friends
on Naboo."

But as usual, Jar Jar chose not to be careful.
He instead started jumping up and down and

making wild animal sounds like those coming from the swamp.

After a moment, more loud and crazy sounds came from the trees in the swamp.

"Oh, dear," was all C-3PO could say as a shower of fruit came flying at them from the trees.

"Dis'n is a different swamp altogether," Jar Jar said as he tried to dodge the flying fruit.

CHAPTER 3

Suddenly, the crazy noises and the flying fruit came to a stop. The swamp went silent. Jar Jar and C-3PO turned to see the doors of the hangar rumble open. They expected to see Padmé coming back to the ship, but instead a squad of four battle droids entered the hangar.

Battle droids served under Count Dooku and the Separatist Alliance, the enemy of the Galactic Republic. Jar Jar and C-3PO were in trouble.

"Stop where you are!" one of the battle droids

said in a metallic, computerized voice.

Jar Jar turned and ran up the ramp and back into the ship. Once inside, he pressed the button on the control panel that raised the ramp.

"Wait for me!" C-3PO said. He was a droid and couldn't move very fast.

As the ramp was closing, Jar Jar reached out and grabbed C-3PO by his metallic arm to try and pull him into the ship. But Jar Jar tripped, as usual, and tumbled out of the ship. He and C-3PO crashed onto the platform. The ramp closed behind them. They were locked out.

C-3PO looked up at Jar Jar, who was sitting on top of him. Again! "Jar Jar, you great webfoot!" he said. "You're squashing my circuits!"

They had almost forgotten about the battle droids, until they heard, "Blast 'em!"

Blaster fire started flying by Jar Jar's and C-3PO's heads. Jar Jar jumped up and ran off.

"Wait! Where are you going?" C-3PO said, not knowing why Jar Jar had left him alone.

As Jar Jar ran off, one of his feet became tangled in a power cord. He tried to get free, but the cord was wrapped around a lever on one of the control consoles on the platform. Jar Jar jerked at the cord and it moved the lever into the "on" position. Lights started to flash and a motor began to hum.

Jar Jar had activated a giant crane. On the end of the crane was a giant metal disc. The disc began to lower very quickly and C-3PO was lying on his back right under it.

"Oh, no! I'll be crushed for sure," C-3PO said nervously as he lay helpless on the ground.

"Hang on, Three-so!" Jar Jar yelled as he dodged blaster fire and started hitting buttons on the control console. Suddenly, the disc stopped.

C-3PO sat up. "That was close!" he said. Just then he saw Jar Jar jerk on the cord once more and it pulled the lever into a third position. C-3PO looked up to see the metal disc start to shake. All of a sudden, C-3PO was pulled off the ground and smashed back-first into the disc. *Clank!* It was a giant magnet and C-3PO was stuck to it.

Jar Jar started pulling all the levers on the console to try and get C-3PO down. He pulled on one and the whole crane started to move. The giant magnet with C-3PO stuck to it started to swing back and forth.

The sound of the oncoming battle droids was getting closer. Jar Jar looked up just in time to see the magnet swing into all four battle droids.

They were smashed to bits.

"Oh, look out, Jar Jar! A crab droid is headed right for you!" C-3PO yelled from the swinging magnet.

"Headed for meesa?" Jar Jar replied.

"Yes, yousa!" C-3PO said. He was getting really annoyed with Jar Jar.

Jar Jar tried to make a run for it, but the crab droid was really fast. He ran around Padmé's ship but found himself up against the edge of the hangar. Below him was a long drop into the jungle.

The crab droid lunged forward with a large mechanical claw. Jar Jar couldn't do anything except grab on to it. The droid pulled its claw back and Jar Jar was thrown onto its back.

Then it started walking in circles and rose up onto its back legs to shake Jar Jar loose. But with the extra weight of Jar Jar on its back, it lost its balance and fell backward and off of the edge of the platform.

C-3PO was still stuck to the magnet and couldn't do anything but watch as the droid and Jar Jar fell from sight.

"Jar Jar! Oh, no! Jar Jar's been killed!" C-3PO cried. "I knew something like this would happen."

CHAPTER 4

"What a horrible way to die," C-3PO moaned as he swung from the magnet. "And it's all my fault. He was so brave. Now he's gone . . . forever."

A moment later he saw a familiar hand climb up from the edge of the platform. It was Jar Jar. He was alive!

"Meesa okay . . ." he said as he fell to the ground, exhausted.

"Well, if you've finished messing around,"

C-3PO snapped. "I need help!"

Jar Jar got up and went to the control console. He looked at it for a moment and then picked a button to press. What luck! The magnet shut off and C-3PO crashed to the ground with a clank.

Wanting to make sure that everything was shut off, Jar Jar flipped one of the levers. All of a sudden the magnet swung over toward Padmé's

ship and then dropped. It smashed right into the cockpit.

"Well," C-3PO said, looking over at Jar Jar. "That's the end of our ship. Typical."

"One thing for sure," Jar Jar added. "Mistress Padmé no liken this."

A little bit later, Jar Jar and C-3PO stood in the wrecked cockpit of Padmé's ship. Sparks from the destroyed command console shot up around them.

"Theesa one big mess! Weesa going nowhere," Jar Jar said as he poked through the remains. "Oh, looky! Here's a button that's still working."

Jar Jar pushed the button and a small closet opened. He walked over and looked inside.

"Thatsa looken like a Jedi robe," he said. "Whosa you supos'n dis belongs to?"

"I wouldn't know, but our only hope is to hide in this closet until Mistress Padmé returns," C-3PO said, moving toward the closet.

Jar Jar couldn't just stay in the ship and hide. He knew that Padmé needed his help. "If those droids attacken us," he said, getting excited, "then Padmé's probably in trouble!"

Jar Jar suddenly grabbed the robe and started to put it on. "We musta hafta try'n saven her," he announced proudly.

C-3PO stood and watched Jar Jar try to get the robe on over his giant ears. "Jar Jar Binks," he said. "Have you gone completely mad? You'll do more harm than good!"

CHAPTER 5

Jar Jar and C-3PO made their way out of the ship and across the hangar.

C-3PO nervously looked around. "Oh, battle droids will surely capture you . . . or worse . . . me."

"Not wit thisa on," Jar Jar said while adjusting the Jedi robe. "Theysa won't be recognizin' me."

C-3PO looked at Jar Jar and just said, "You can't be serious."

Jar Jar didn't care. He knew Padmé needed him. "Come on, Three-so, we can do it!"

"I have a very bad feeling about this," C-3PO called to Jar Jar as he followed him across the hangar and into the courtyard.

Just then a giant, dark shadow passed over them. They looked up and saw a Separatist shuttle heading for the hangar. Jar Jar and C-3PO moved into the shadows and waited until the shuttle landed.

It was Nute Gunray. He was the Viceroy of

the Trade Federation and one of the heads of the Separatist Alliance. And he had brought along many more battle droids. *Vissa Gunray'sa badn man*, Jar Jar thought. *Meesa knowin' Mistress Padmé is in muy muy troublin'.*

Coming to meet the Viceroy was Senator Onaconda Farr, who was Padmé's old friend and the one they had come to meet. Jar Jar wanted to warn him that Nute Gunray was a bad guy and that he should be careful. But before Jar Jar could do anything, Senator Farr said something unexpected. "We are holding Senator Amidala in the detention tower."

What? Jar Jar couldn't believe what he was hearing. Padmé was in bigger trouble than he had thought.

Jar Jar looked at C-3PO and pointed up at the detention tower. "Mistress Padmé's up in that tower? Weesa gotta rescue'n her."

C-3PO started to complain about Jar Jar's plan, but then they heard the metallic voice of a battle droid. "Look! A Jedi!"

A Jedi! Weesa saved, Jar Jar thought. He lifted his head to see who it was. Maybe it was Anakin Skywalker. He was a good friend of Padmé's and always came to her rescue.

"Where'sa Jedi?" Jar Jar asked. He couldn't see any Jedi.

C-3PO let out a sigh. "I do believe they mean you!" The battle droids thought Jar Jar was a Jedi because he was wearing the robe he found in Padmé's ship.

"Meesa no Jedi!" Jar Jar screamed as he ran from the battle droid's blaster fire. But it was too late. One of the laser blasts hit him. When the smoke cleared there was nothing left but the Jedi cloak. Jar Jar was gone.

CHAPTER 6

Jar Jar splashed into the swamp. He had snuck through a grate in the platform and landed in the dark water below.

Meesa safe, he thought as he stood up deep below the surface of the swamp. Luckily, Jar Jar could breath underwater. He went to take a step, but the floor of the swamp began to move. Jar Jar looked down at his feet to see what was happening. He couldn't see anything, so he took a closer look. Just then a giant eye opened up right under his feet.

He wasn't standing on the floor of the swamp, he was standing on a giant swamp monster.

"Dersa bad boogie monster down here!" Jar Jar screamed as the monster swung around to chomp at him. Jar Jar had spent most of his life underwater and was a really good swimmer, so he was able to get out of the way of the monster's giant jaws.

Jar Jar swam away as fast as he could. Once he was safe from the monster, he climbed up a tall pole and back out of the grate. He still had

to get to the tower and rescue Padmé.

On the platform, Jar Jar looked around for C-3PO, but his metal friend was gone. He was afraid that the battle droids had captured him. Jar Jar picked up the Jedi robe and put it back on. He needed his disguise to get into the tower. The door was blocked by battle droids, so Jar Jar decided that he would climb up the outside of the tower. There were giant vines up and down the sides of the tower, and Jar Jar thought that he

could use those to get to Padmé's cell.

Jar Jar climbed higher and higher up the tower. He could hear someone talking on a balcony above him, so he stopped and peeked his head over the edge to take a look. It was Nute Gunray.

"Bring Senator Amidala before me," Gunray ordered a battle droid.

The droid replied nervously, "She has escaped, sir."

"Escaped!" Jar Jar gasped loudly. He was

so happy that Padmé had gotten away that he forgot that he was hiding.

The battle droid looked over and saw Jar Jar's head. "It's the Jedi!" he yelled.

Gunray looked at Jar Jar and ordered the battle droid to shoot at him.

As Jar Jar moved his head to avoid the blaster fire, his hands slipped and he fell backward off of the wall.

"Ahhhhhhhhhhhhh!" he screamed as he wildly

began to swing his arms and legs around.

The courtyard below was getting closer and closer. Jar Jar was getting really scared, and then he just stopped falling. Something had grabbed his foot. It was a vine. He had somehow gotten his foot tangled up in it as he was falling.

"Theesa rescuin' is hard jobbin'!" he said as he swung back and forth.

Jar Jar looked down at the ground. It was only a few feet below him. He felt very lucky that the vine had saved him. Suddenly, more blaster fire came at him from the battle droids on the balcony. He tried to shake his foot free as a laser blast hit the vine and cut it in half. Jar Jar dropped to the ground and landed on his head.

He stood up quickly and shook it off. He turned to run, but it was too late. Battle droids were coming at him from all directions.

CHAPTER 7

Jar Jar only had one choice. He had to climb back through the grate and into the swamp with the giant monster. He splashed down into the water and swam to safety. Above the grate, battle droids shot down into the water at him.

Then Jar Jar heard a sound. A plunk. The battle droids had dropped something into the water. Jar Jar could see it coming toward him. It was a grenade and it was set to explode!

Jar Jar didn't know what to do, so he grabbed

the grenade and swam to the surface of the water. He had just one chance to save himself. He concentrated, and with all his might, threw the grenade back up at the grate.

He couldn't believe it. The grenade went right through and landed on the platform! *Meesa wonderin' why things like this never a'happen when Three-so's around,* Jar Jar thought. No one would ever believe him.

A second later there was an explosion. Small bits of destroyed droids came through the grate and landed in the water. Then he heard another plunk. Then another. *Plunk. Plunk. Plunk.* Dozens of grenades had been dropped into the water.

Jar Jar's eyes went wide and he swam off as fast as he could. The grenades were exploding behind him, but he was far enough away. He looked back at the explosions and saw something coming at him. It was a missile!

One of the battle droids shot a missile at him and it was coming quickly. Jar Jar was afraid that he wasn't a fast enough swimmer to get away. He swam as hard as he could, but the missile always seemed to be right behind him.

Just then, Jar Jar saw his chance to get away. There was a sharp corner up ahead. If he moved quickly he could get around it before the missile hit him.

It had been a while since Jar Jar had swam this much, but he was moving like he'd never been out of the water. The turn was coming up and Jar Jar knew just what to do. At the last minute he kicked his legs and his body sailed easily around the corner.

But as Jar Jar rounded the corner he saw a giant pair of eyes staring at him. It was the swamp monster!

"Bogey!" Jar Jar screamed as he turned and

swam back in the other direction.

The missile was coming right at him and the swamp monster was right behind him. Jar Jar didn't know what to do. All of a sudden the giant mouth of the monster came crashing around him. Just as its teeth clamped down, Jar Jar heard an explosion. The missile had hit the swamp monster.

Jar Jar was tossed back and forth in the creature's mouth. It was dark and wet and Jar Jar was scared.

Suddenly the monster stopped moving. Jar Jar stood up and tried to pull the creature's giant mouth open. It was really hard, but Jar Jar was able to get its teeth apart and swim through.

The swamp monster looked at Jar Jar and tried to move, but it was trapped under debris from the explosion. Jar Jar swam over to the monster and smiled.

"Yousa okay, bogey?" he said. "Yousa savin' me. Yousa my new palo."

CHAPTER 8

Meesa friends in trouble, Jar Jar thought as he swam off to find Padmé and C-3PO.

Jar Jar kept swimming until he heard a familiar voice coming from a grate above the swamp. "I say, I think there's been some horrible mistake!" It was C-3PO!

Jar Jar climbed up and looked out of the grate. He could see Padmé and C-3PO. Nute Gunray and Senator Farr had them trapped against a wall. There were three destroyer droids with their blasters aimed at them.

Jar Jar climbed out from the grate, pulled the hood of the Jedi robe up over his head, and stood as tall as he could.

Senator Farr looked at Jar Jar and screamed, "It's the Jedi!"

Padmé smiled at Jar Jar and, even though he was afraid, he knew that he had done the right thing.

"Release da Sentah!" Jar Jar said, trying to sound as much like a Jedi as he could.

All the battle droids turned and pointed their blasters at him.

"Shoot him!" Gunray ordered.

Then, with a mighty roar, the swamp monster burst up from below the grate. Jar Jar was thrown in the air and landed on the monster's back. The battle droids were all knocked to the ground.

"The Jedi has summoned a monster!" Gunray screamed as he ran off.

Padmé chased after Gunray as he made his way to the hangar. He was trying to get away in his shuttle. Jar Jar and the swamp monster were right behind them.

Jar Jar did the best he could to hold on, but his new friend had a mind of its own and wanted to get back to the swamp. The swamp monster roared as it made its way through the hangar and finally threw Jar Jar from its back.

Jar Jar landed on the ground as the swamp

monster smashed into Gunray's shuttle, knocking it into the swamp.

"Hold it right there, Viceroy," Padmé said to Gunray. Her blaster was pointed right at him.

Gunray turned to run, but he was blocked by Jedi Jar Jar. There was nowhere for him to go. He was trapped.

A short while later the clone army arrived. They were there to arrest Viceroy Gunray for trying to kidnap Padmé. As the clone commander exited his ship, he saw Jar Jar in the Jedi robe and saluted him.

"What are your orders, General?" the clone commander asked Jar Jar.

C-3PO gave Jar Jar a confused look. He just couldn't believe how anyone could mistake Jar Jar for a Jedi, especially a clone commander.

With the mission over, Padmé received another holographic message from Chancellor Palpatine.

"The capture of Viceroy Gunray is a major victory for the Republic," the Chancellor said. "All of you should be commended for your courage, and from what I hear, especially you, Representative Jar Jar Binks."

Jar Jar stood proudly next to Padmé and C-3PO. He may not have been a Jedi, but he knew he was a hero.